Woof moves to the City

Om KIDZ
An imprint of Om Books International

Om KIDZ | Om Books International

Reprinted in 2024

Corporate & Editorial Office
A-12, Sector 64, Noida 201 301
Uttar Pradesh, India
Phone: +91 120 477 4100
Email: editorial@ombooks.com
Website: www.ombooksinternational.com

Sales Office
107, Ansari Road, Darya Ganj
New Delhi 110 002, India
Phone: +91 11 4000 9000
Email: sales@ombooks.com
Website: www.ombooks.com

ISBN: 978-93-84625-12-2

Printed in India

10 9 8 7 6

Woof moves to the city

I'm all set to read

Paste your photograph here

My name is

Woof was a happy dog. He lived a happy life in the countryside.

He lived with a farmer by the corn fields. The farmer fed him well. He would bask in the sun every day and stare into the starry sky at night.

The cows and buffaloes who ploughed the fields, the horses, the hen and her chicks, and the furry brown cat were Woof's friends. The cat ate the mice in Woof's fields too.

The best part about his life? The farmer never put a leash on him. He roamed about freely.

"Come on, Woof. It's time to go," the farmer said Woof one afternoon. Woof was running around with his friends. He stopped and looked up at the farmer. "We're moving to the city. I need to sell my crop and make more money," said the farmer.

The car tyres rolled on the dusty country roads. Woof looked out of the car to see the fields, the house and his friends. He was leaving all of them and moving to the city. Woof cried in the backseat.

The city was nothing like Woof had ever seen. There were many tall buildings and very few trees. There were so many cars everywhere!

There were lots of people and a lot of noise! Woof was amazed to see so much all at once. It was very different from the countryside.

Woof had to get into an elevator to reach his house. The elevator scared him, but not as much as the house did. He was so high up that from his house, everything else looked really tiny. The farmer and Woof lived alone in the apartment.

At night, when he looked out of the window, he saw colourful blinking lights. It was nothing like the starry night he saw from his fields.

Woof missed the fields and his friends. He longed to go home.

Days passed and Woof slowly learned how to live in the city.

Every morning, he would go with the farmer to the Fresh Market. The farmer did not put a leash on him like other people did to their dogs. He knew that Woof would never leave him!

In the evenings, after returning from the market, the farmer would take Woof for a walk.

Woof learnt how to cross the road too. He looked to his right, then to his left and always crossed at the zebra crossing. He learnt how to read signals and signboards too!

Woof and the farmer would go to the park, where the farmer would meet his friends. Some of them brought their dogs along, too. Woof started to make new friends. They would play “catch the ball” and “dog and the bone”.

Woof would run around the park with his friends. They would fetch a ball, play hide and seek and chase each other.

At night, he would return to his house, get into the elevator and back into his apartment.

The farmer would fill up his feeding bowl and Woof would happily eat it all!

Woof was starting to like the city life.

He had new friends. He learnt new things. People greeted him when he went to the market or for walks.

The city lights at night reminded him of starry skies over the fields!

coffee
CLIO

"Come on, Woof! It's time to go," the farmer told Woof as he packed his bags one day.

Woof was confused. "We're going for a vacation to the countryside!" said the farmer as he hugged Woof. Woof ran around in circles and wagged his tail happily!

Woof and the farmer drove to the countryside. His friends were thrilled to meet him.

Woof told them all about his city life and they told them about their days without him.

Woof enjoyed being in the fields for a few days. Soon, it was time to go back to the city.

"I have the best of both worlds – the country side and the city," said Woof as he smiled and wagged his tail.